HORRID HENRY'S
Christmas Lunch

HORRiD HENRY'S
Christmas Lunch

Francesca Simon
Illustrated by Tony Ross

Orion
Children's Books

Horrid Henry's Christmas Lunch originally appeared in
Horrid Henry's Christmas Cracker, first published in
Great Britain in 2006 by Orion Children's Books
This edition first published in Great Britain in 2014
by Orion Children's Books
a division of the Orion Publishing Group Ltd
Orion House
5 Upper Saint Martin's Lane
London WC2H 9EA
An Hachette UK Company

1 3 5 7 9 10 8 6 4 2

The Orion Publishing Group's policy is to use papers that
are natural, renewable and recyclable products and made
from wood grown in sustainable forests. The logging and
manufacturing processes are expected to conform to the
environmental regulations of the country of origin.

A catalogue record for this book is available from the British Library.

ISBN 978 1 4440 0124 2
Printed in China

www.orionbooks.co.uk
www.horridhenry.co.uk

There are many more **Horrid Henry** books available.
For a complete list visit
www.horridhenry.co.uk
or
www.orionbooks.co.uk

Contents

Chapter 1

"Oh, handkerchiefs, just what
I wanted," said Perfect Peter.
"Thank you *so* much."

"Not handkerchiefs again," moaned Horrid Henry, throwing the hankies aside and ripping the paper off the next present in his pile.

"Don't tear the wrapping paper!"
squeaked Perfect Peter.
Horrid Henry ripped open the
present and groaned.

Yuck (a pen, pencil, and ruler).

Yuck (a dictionary).

Yuck (gloves).

OK
(£15 – should have been a lot more).

Eeeew
(a pink bow tie from Aunt Ruby).

Eeeeew (mints).

Yum (huge tin of chocolates).

Good
(five more
knights for
his army).

Very good
(a subscription to
Gross-Out Fan
Club)…

And (very very good)
a Terminator Gladiator trident …

And…
And … where was the rest?
"Is that it?" shrieked Henry.

"You haven't opened
my present, Henry," said Peter.
"I hope you like it."

Horrid Henry tore off the wrapping.
It was a Manners With Maggie
calendar.

"Ugh, gross," said Henry.
"No thank you."

"Henry!" said Mum.
"That's no way to receive a present."

"I don't care," moaned Horrid Henry. "Where's my Zapatron Hip-Hop dinosaur? And where's the rest of the Terminator Gladiator fighting kit? I wanted everything, not just the trident."

"Maybe next year," said Mum.

"But I want it now!" howled Henry.

"Henry, you know that
'I want doesn't get'," said Peter.
"Isn't that right, Mum?"

"It certainly is," said Mum. "And
I haven't heard you say thank you,
Henry."

Horrid Henry glared at Peter
and sprang. He was a hornet
stinging a worm to death.

"WAAAAAAH!"
wailed Peter.

"Henry! Stop it or…"

DING! DONG!

Chapter 2

"They're here!" shouted Horrid Henry, leaping up and abandoning his prey. "That means more presents!"

"Wait, Henry," said Mum.

But too late. Henry raced to the door
and flung it open.

There stood Granny and Grandpa,
Prissy Polly, Pimply Paul, and
Vomiting Vera.

"Gimme my presents!" he shrieked, snatching a bag of brightly wrapped gifts out of Granny's hand and spilling them on the floor. Now, where were the ones with his name on?

"Merry Christmas, everyone,"
said Mum brightly.
"Henry, don't be rude."

"I'm not being rude, I just want
my presents. Great, money!" said
Henry, beaming. "Thanks, Granny!
But couldn't you add a few pounds
and –"

"Henry, don't be horrid!" snapped Dad.

"Let the guests take off their coats," said Mum.

"Bleeeeech," said Vomiting Vera, throwing up on Paul.

"Eeeeek," said Polly.

★

All the grown-ups gathered in the
sitting room to open their gifts.

"Peter, thank you so much for the perfume, it's my favourite," said Granny.

"I know," said Peter.

"And what a lovely comic, Henry,"
said Granny. "Mutant Max is my …
um … favourite."

"Thank you, Henry," said Grandpa.
"This comic looks very …
interesting."

"I'll have it back when you've
finished with it," said Henry.

"Henry!" said Mum, glaring.

For some reason Polly didn't look
delighted with her present.
"Eeeek!" squeaked Polly.
"This soap has ... hairs in it."
She pulled out a long black one.

"That came free," said Horrid Henry.

"We're getting you toothpaste next
year, you little brat," muttered Pimply
Paul under his breath.

Honestly, there was no pleasing some people, thought Horrid Henry indignantly. He'd given Paul a great bar of soap, and he didn't seem thrilled. So much for it's the thought that counts.

Chapter 3

"A poem," said Mum.
"Henry, how lovely."

"Read it out loud," said Grandpa.

'Dear old wrinkley Mum
Don't be glum
'Cause you've got a fat tum
And an even bigger...'

"Maybe later," said Mum.

"Another poem," said Dad. "Great!"

"Let's hear it," said Granny.

'Dear old baldy Dad—

...and so forth," said Dad, folding
Henry's poem quickly.

"Oh," said Polly, staring at the crystal frog vase Mum and Dad had given her. "How funny. This looks just like the vase I gave Aunt Ruby for Christmas last year."

"What a coincidence," said Mum, blushing bright red.

"Great minds think alike," said Dad quickly.

Dad gave Mum an iron.
"Oh, an iron, just what I always
wanted," said Mum.

Mum gave Dad oven gloves.
"Oh, oven gloves, just what I always
wanted," said Dad.

Pimply Paul gave Prissy Polly
a huge power drill.
"Eeeek," squealed Polly.
"What's this?"

"Oh, that's the Megawatt Superduper
Drill-o-matic 670 XM3," said
Paul, "and just wait till you see the
attachments. You're getting those
for your birthday."

"Oh," said Polly.

Granny gave Grandpa a lovely mug
to put his false teeth in.

Grandpa gave Granny a shower cap
and a bumper pack of dusters.

"What super presents!" said Mum.

"Yes," said Perfect Peter. "I loved every single one of my presents, especially the satsumas and walnuts in my stocking."

"I didn't," said Horrid Henry.

"Henry, don't be horrid," said Dad. "Who'd like a mince pie?"

"Are they homemade or from the shop?" asked Henry.

"Homemade of course," said Dad.

"Gross," said Henry.

"Ooh," said Polly. "No, Vera!" she squealed as Vera vomited all over the plate.

"Never mind," said Mum tightly. "There's more in the kitchen."

Chapter 4

Horrid Henry was bored.
Horrid Henry was fed up.

The presents had all been opened. His parents had made him go on a long, boring walk.

Dad had confiscated his Terminator trident when he had speared Peter with it. So, what now?

Grandpa was sitting in the armchair
with his pipe, snoring, his tinsel
crown slipping over his face.

Prissy Polly and Pimply Paul were
squabbling over whose turn it was
to change Vera's stinky nappy.
"Eeeek," said Polly. "I did it last."

"I did," said Paul.

"WAAAAAAAA!"
wailed Vomiting Vera.

Perfect Peter was watching Sammy
the Snail slithering about on TV.
Horrid Henry snatched the clicker
and switched channels.
"Hey, I was watching that!"
protested Peter.

"Tough," said Henry.

Let's see, what was on?
"Tra la la la…"
Ick!
Daffy and her Dancing Daisies.

"Wait! I want to watch!"
wailed Peter.

Click.

"… and the tension builds as the
judges compare tomatoes grown…"

Click!

"… wish you a Merry Christmas,
we wish you…"

Click!

"Chartres Cathedral is one of the wonders of…"

Click!

"HA HA HA HA HA HA HA HA."
Opera!

Click!

Why was there nothing good on TV?
Just a baby movie about singing cars
he'd seen a million times already.

"I'm bored," moaned Henry.
"And I'm starving."
He wandered into the kitchen,
which looked like a hurricane
had swept through.
"When's lunch? I thought we were
eating at two. I'm starving."

"Soon," said Mum.
She looked a little frazzled.
"There's been a little problem
with the oven."

"So when's lunch?"
bellowed Horrid Henry.

"When it's ready!" bellowed Dad.

Chapter 5

Henry waited.
And waited.
And waited.

"When's lunch?" asked Polly.

"When's lunch?" asked Paul.

"When's lunch?" asked Peter.

"As soon as the turkey is cooked,"
said Dad. He peeked into the oven.
He poked the turkey.
Then he went pale.
"It's hardly cooked," he whispered.

"Check the temperature,"
said Granny.

Dad checked.
"Oops," said Dad.

"Never mind, we can start with the
sprouts," said Mum cheerfully.

"That's not the right way to do sprouts," said Granny. "You're peeling too many of the leaves off."

"Yes, Mother," said Dad.

"That's not the right way to make bread sauce," said Granny.

"Yes, Mother," said Dad.

"That's not the right way to make stuffing," said Granny.

"Yes, Mother," said Dad.

"That's not the right way to roast potatoes," said Granny.

"Mother!" yelped Dad.
"Leave me alone!"

"Don't be horrid," said Granny.

"I'm not being horrid," said Dad.

"Come along, Granny, let's get you a nice drink and leave the chef on his own," said Mum, steering Granny firmly towards the sitting room. Then she stopped.

"Is something burning?"
asked Mum, sniffing.

Dad checked the oven.
"Not in here."

There was a shriek from
the sitting room.
"It's Grandpa!" shouted
Perfect Peter.

Everyone ran in.

There was Grandpa, asleep in his chair. A thin column of black smoke rose from the arms. His paper crown, drooping over his pipe, was smoking.

"Whh…whh?" mumbled Grandpa, as Mum whacked him with her broom.

"AAARRGH!" he gurgled as Dad threw water over him.

"When's lunch?"
screamed Horrid Henry.

"When it's ready," screamed Dad.

Chapter 6

It was dark when Henry's family
finally sat down to Christmas lunch.

Henry's tummy was rumbling
so loudly with hunger he thought
the walls would cave in.

Henry and Peter made a dash
to grab the seat against the wall,
furthest from the kitchen.

"Get off!" shouted Henry.

"It's my turn to sit here,"
wailed Peter.

"Mine!"

"Mine!"

Slap!

Slap!

"Waaaaaaaaaa!"
screeched Henry.

"Waaaaaaaaaa!"
wailed Peter.

"Quiet!"
screamed Dad.

Mum brought in fresh holly
and ivy to decorate the table.
"Lovely," said Mum, placing the
boughs all along the centre.

"Very festive," said Granny.

"I'm starving!" wailed Horrid Henry.
"This isn't Christmas lunch,
it's Christmas dinner."

"Shhh," said Grandpa.

The turkey was finally cooked.
There were platefuls of stuffing,
sprouts, cranberries, bread sauce
and peas.
"Smells good," said Granny.

"Hmmn, boy," said Grandpa.
"What a feast."

Horrid Henry was so hungry he
could eat the tablecloth.
"Come on, let's eat!" he said.

"Hold on, I'll just get the roast
potatoes," said Dad. Wearing his
new oven gloves, he carried in the
steaming hot potatoes in a glass
roasting dish, and set it in the
middle of the table.

"*Voila!*" said Dad. "Now, who wants
dark meat and who…"

"What's that crawling …

aaaarrrghh!"

screamed Polly.
"There are spiders everywhere!"

Millions of tiny spiders were pouring from the holly and crawling all over the table and the food.

"Don't panic!" shouted Pimply Paul,
leaping from his chair. "I know what
to do, we just –"
But before he could do anything
the glass dish with the roast potatoes
exploded.

Crash!

Smash!

"EEEEEKK!" screamed Polly.

Everyone stared at the slivers
of glass glistening all over the table
and the food.
Dad sank down in his chair
and covered his eyes.

"Where are we going to get more
food?" whispered Mum.

"I don't know," muttered Dad.

"I know," said Horrid Henry. "Let's start with Christmas pudding and defrost some pizzas."

Dad opened his eyes.
Mum opened her eyes.
"That," said Dad, "is a brilliant idea."

"I really fancy some pizza,"
said Grandpa.

"Me too," said Granny.

Henry beamed.
It wasn't often his ideas were
recognised for their brilliance.

"Merry Christmas, everyone,"
said Horrid Henry.
"Merry Christmas."